Baby the Vampire Terrier

Baby the Vampire Terrier

Matthew Petchinsky

Baby the Vampire Terrier
By: Matthew Petchinsky

Introduction: Baby, the Adorable Vampire Boston Terrier of Moonlit Hollow

Nestled in the heart of a quaint, sleepy town lies a place unlike any other—a town called Moonlit Hollow. Famous for its cobblestone streets, charming cottages, and the perpetual glow of its silvery moonlight, it feels like a place where magic lingers just beneath the surface. Here, among the rustling trees and glowing lanterns, lives Baby, a Boston Terrier like no other.

At first glance, Baby seems like your typical Boston Terrier: small, perky, and irresistibly adorable. Her sleek black-and-white coat gleams in the moonlight, and her wide, soulful eyes are full of curiosity and warmth. She has an irresistible charm, one that has made her a beloved fixture of Moonlit Hollow. The townsfolk adore her for her playful antics and boundless energy. From chasing butterflies in the meadow to greeting every passerby with a wagging tail, Baby is the heartbeat of joy in this cozy town.

But Baby has a tiny secret—a secret that not even her closest friends suspect. She's a vampire. That's right! Beneath her sweet exterior lies a nocturnal creature of the night with powers most would find extraordinary—and perhaps even a little frightening. Yet, Baby isn't the kind of vampire you see in old stories or scary movies. She doesn't haunt dark castles or drink blood under the cover of night. Instead, Baby uses her unique abilities for good—or at least for a little harmless mischief.

Baby's vampire powers are as unique as she is. With her heightened senses, she can hear the faintest whispers of a squirrel plotting to steal acorns or the soft rustle of leaves as the wind whispers through the trees. Her speed is unmatched, allowing her to dash through Moonlit Hollow in the blink of an eye, leaving a trail of giggles and astonished gasps behind her. She can even float, a skill she often uses to reach high shelves or to snag a snack that's just out of paw's reach. And let's not forget her hypnotic gaze—though she mostly uses it to charm her way to extra treats or an extra-long belly rub.

Moonlit Hollow is the perfect setting for Baby's adventures. The town is alive with whimsical characters and enchanting mysteries. There's Mrs. Whiskerbee, the elderly baker whose pies are said to have a hint of magic; Jasper, the mischievous black cat who claims to know every secret the town holds; and the friendly but peculiar twins, Ivy and Oliver, who are always on the hunt for their next great discovery. Together, they form a community that is as delightful as it is intriguing, and Baby is at the heart of it all.

But Baby's vampire nature isn't just about powers and fun. It also means she's awake when most of Moonlit Hollow is fast asleep. The nighttime becomes her playground, a time when she explores the mysteries of the moonlit world, lending a paw where she's needed and finding adventure around every corner. Whether it's helping a lost hedgehog find its way home, uncovering a hidden treasure, or solving the mystery of the flickering streetlamp, Baby's nights are never boring.

Yet, despite her secret, Baby longs for connection and friendship. She cherishes her human companions and animal friends, even if they don't know her full story. For Baby, being a vampire isn't a curse; it's a part of who she is—a tiny part of her big, lovable personality. And while she sometimes worries about what others might think if they discovered her secret, she knows that her heart is as warm as the sun she rarely sees.

As you turn the pages of Baby's tale, you'll be whisked away to Moonlit Hollow, where every shadow holds a story, and every moonbeam lights the way to a new adventure. You'll laugh at Baby's playful antics, cheer for her daring exploits, and maybe, just maybe, find yourself believing in the magic of the night.

So, get ready to meet Baby, the Boston Terrier with a heart full of love, a streak of mischief, and a secret as magical as the moonlit town she calls home. Welcome to Moonlit Hollow, where the nights are lively, the friendships are unbreakable, and the adventures never end.

Chapter 1: Baby's Big Secret

The night was quiet in Moonlit Hollow, the kind of quiet that made the faintest sounds seem louder. Crickets chirped their rhythmic tune, and the soft rustle of leaves in the gentle breeze filled the air. In the quaint little cottage at the edge of town, Baby, the lovable Boston Terrier, lay curled up on her favorite blanket by the fireplace. She had spent the day chasing her tail, nosing through fallen leaves, and charming everyone she encountered. As far as Baby knew, it had been a perfectly ordinary day.

But tonight, something felt different.

Baby woke suddenly, her ears perking up at a sound she couldn't quite place. She tilted her head, listening intently. It wasn't the usual creak of the old wooden floors or the distant hoot of an owl. No, this sound was sharper, clearer—like the faint rustle of fabric far away. Her heart raced as she realized she could pinpoint exactly where the sound was coming from: the upstairs bedroom. Lucy, her beloved owner, was tossing and turning in her sleep.

Baby blinked in surprise. Since when could she hear so clearly? She shook her head, assuming it was just her imagination. But when she leaped down from her blanket, she noticed something else. Her landing was silent—completely silent. Usually, her tiny paws made a soft thud against the floor. She tested it again, hopping from one spot to another, and each time, no sound.

Curious, Baby trotted over to the hallway mirror, her reflection illuminated by the faint glow of moonlight streaming through the window. As she looked into the mirror, something caught her eye. She moved closer, her black-and-white face tilting in confusion. There, gleaming ever so slightly under her lips, were two tiny fangs.

Her eyes widened, and she barked in alarm—a sound that seemed almost too loud in the stillness of the night. She pawed at her mouth, her nails clicking gently against her muzzle. The fangs were unmistakable, small but sharp, and they hadn't been there yesterday.

Baby backed away from the mirror, her little heart thumping in her chest. What was happening to her? She looked down at her paws, half-expecting them to change too, but they looked normal enough. Testing another theory, she bounded toward the kitchen, aiming for the countertop where Lucy kept the cookie jar. Normally, the counter was far out of reach, even with her best jump. But this time, Baby leaped—and soared higher than she'd ever imagined. She landed gracefully on the countertop, staring down at the cookie jar in awe.

Her tail wagged furiously. This was amazing!

Forgetting her initial fear, Baby hopped back to the floor with ease. She dashed around the house, testing her newfound agility. She leaped over the couch, bounded up the stairs in two effortless jumps, and landed softly on Lucy's bed without waking her. Every leap and bound felt like pure magic.

However, her excitement was short-lived as questions filled her mind. How had she gained these powers? Was it something she ate? Something in the water? And what would Lucy think if she found out?

Baby trotted back downstairs and curled up on her blanket, her little fangs still poking out from beneath her lips. She tried to fall back asleep, but the excitement and confusion kept her awake until morning.

The next day, Baby decided she couldn't keep this secret to herself. Lucy was her best friend, and if anyone could help her make sense of this, it was Lucy. As Lucy poured herself a cup of coffee and prepared Baby's breakfast, Baby sat at her feet, wagging her tail nervously.

"Morning, Baby!" Lucy said, reaching down to scratch behind Baby's ears. "You're up early today."

Baby barked in response and then jumped onto the kitchen counter, landing softly beside the coffee pot. Lucy gasped, nearly dropping her mug.

"Baby! How—what—did you just—jump? Onto the counter?" Lucy's wide eyes stared at her in disbelief.

Baby wagged her tail sheepishly and gave her best puppy-dog eyes. Then, as if to explain, she opened her mouth slightly, letting her fangs glint in the morning light.

Lucy froze, her coffee forgotten. "Are those...fangs?" she whispered. "Baby, what's going on?"

Baby barked again, hopping down from the counter to sit at Lucy's feet. She tilted her head, as if to say, *I don't know either!*

Lucy crouched down, looking Baby in the eye. "This is...weird. But also kind of cool." She smiled, rubbing Baby's head. "I don't know what's happening, but you're still my Baby, no matter what."

Relieved, Baby licked Lucy's hand, her tail wagging furiously. Lucy laughed and hugged her tightly.

"Alright," Lucy said, pulling back and looking at Baby seriously. "We're going to figure this out. But promise me one thing, Baby. Promise me you'll only use your...uh, new abilities for good."

Baby barked once, loud and confident, as if to say, *You got it!*

Lucy chuckled. "I mean it, Baby. No stealing cookies off the counter or chasing the mailman up a tree. Deal?"

Baby barked again, this time with a hint of mischief. She couldn't promise she wouldn't have a little fun with her powers. After all, what good were super-speed and incredible leaps if she couldn't use them for a prank or two? But she knew Lucy trusted her, and she would do her best to keep that trust.

As the sun rose higher over Moonlit Hollow, Baby felt a new sense of purpose. She didn't know how she'd gotten her powers or why, but she knew one thing for sure: her life was about to get a lot more exciting. And with Lucy by her side, she was ready for whatever adventures lay ahead.

Chapter 2: The Midnight Adventure

The clock struck midnight, its chime echoing softly through Moonlit Hollow. Most of the town was fast asleep, their dreams weaving through the quiet, moonlit streets. But for Baby, this was the perfect time for an adventure.

As she lay curled on her blanket by the hearth, her ears twitched at the faint sounds of the night—the rustling leaves, the distant hoot of an owl, and the soft chirping of crickets. The house was silent, with Lucy asleep upstairs. Baby's mind raced with thoughts of the previous night. Her newfound abilities felt like a gift waiting to be unwrapped, and she couldn't resist the urge to test them further.

Quietly, she padded over to the front door. With a quick glance to ensure Lucy wouldn't wake, she leaped effortlessly to the latch and nudged it open with her nose. The door creaked slightly, and Baby froze, her ears swiveling to listen. When no sound came from upstairs, she slipped out into the cool, moonlit air, the door clicking shut behind her.

The world outside was alive with the magic of the night. The silver moonlight bathed the cobblestone streets, casting long, delicate shadows of the houses and trees. Baby's paws made no sound as she trotted down the road, her sharp senses picking up every detail—the sweet scent of blooming night jasmine, the faint rustle of nocturnal creatures in the bushes, and the distant gurgle of the creek that wound its way through the outskirts of town.

As she wandered, Baby felt a thrill of freedom. She leaped over fences and dashed through open fields, her speed making the world blur around her. The quiet town seemed to open itself up to her in a way it never had before, as though the night itself welcomed her.

Her journey brought her to the edge of town, where the lights of Moonlit Hollow faded, and the forest began. The trees loomed tall and shadowy, their branches intertwining to form a canopy that shimmered with patches of moonlight. Baby hesitated for a moment. The forest had always seemed mysterious and a little intimidating, even during the day. But tonight, it felt different—inviting, almost as though it were calling her.

Gathering her courage, Baby took a tentative step forward, her paws sinking slightly into the soft earth. The air grew cooler, carrying the faint scent of moss and wildflowers. As she ventured deeper, the sounds of the forest surrounded her—the whisper of leaves, the distant croak of frogs, and the occasional crack of a twig underfoot.

Suddenly, a small shadow flitted across her path. Baby stopped in her tracks, her ears perking up. The shadow darted again, this time closer, and she could hear the faint flutter of wings. A moment later, a tiny bat swooped down and hovered in front of her, its beady eyes shining with curiosity.

"Hey there, pup!" the bat squeaked, its voice high-pitched but friendly. "What's a little thing like you doing out here in the middle of the night?"

Baby tilted her head, unsure how to respond. The bat flapped its wings and landed lightly on a low-hanging branch, folding its leathery wings around itself like a cloak.

"The name's Pip," the bat said with a toothy grin. "And you don't look like any ordinary dog to me. Those fangs of yours—well, they're something special."

Baby barked softly, wagging her tail. She hadn't expected to meet anyone on her midnight escapade, let alone a chatty bat.

Pip tilted his head. "Let me guess—you're new to this whole 'creature of the night' thing, huh? Don't worry, I've been doing this for years. Stick with me, and I'll show you the ropes."

Baby barked again, this time with enthusiasm. She liked Pip's energy and decided she could use a guide. The little bat seemed to know the forest well, and his mischievous grin hinted at an adventurous spirit that matched her own.

"Alright then," Pip said, spreading his wings. "Follow me, and I'll show you something really special. But keep up—I'm faster than I look!"

With that, Pip took off, his wings beating rhythmically as he glided through the trees. Baby bounded after him, leaping over fallen logs and weaving through the underbrush. The deeper they went into the forest, the more it seemed to change. The trees grew taller, their trunks glowing faintly with an otherworldly light. The air sparkled with tiny, floating motes that shimmered like stars. Baby's eyes widened in wonder.

They emerged into a clearing, and Baby skidded to a stop, her paws digging into the soft moss. Before her was the most enchanting sight she had ever seen. The clearing was bathed in a soft, golden light that seemed to emanate from the trees themselves. At the center stood a massive oak tree, its trunk gnarled and ancient, with roots that spread out like fingers gripping the earth. Its branches were draped with glowing, silken vines that swayed gently, even though there was no wind.

"Welcome to the Enchanted Grove," Pip announced, landing on a low branch of the oak tree. "Not many get to see this place. It's special—magical."

Baby took a tentative step forward, her nose twitching as she sniffed the air. It smelled sweet, like honey and wildflowers. She could feel the magic of the place humming in the air, a gentle vibration that seemed to resonate with her own newfound powers.

"This grove is ancient," Pip continued. "They say it's the heart of the forest, a place where magic flows strongest. I come here when I need to think—or when I'm looking for a little adventure." He grinned. "And something tells me you're up for a lot of adventures."

Baby barked, her tail wagging furiously. She felt a deep connection to the grove, as though it were welcoming her, inviting her to explore its secrets. The golden light reflected in her eyes, and for the first time, she felt like she truly belonged to the night.

As the moon climbed higher in the sky, Baby and Pip sat together under the ancient oak, their new friendship sealed by the magic of the grove. Baby didn't know what the future held, but she knew one thing for certain—her adventures were just beginning, and with Pip by her side, there was no telling how far they would go.

Chapter 3: A Howling Mystery

The enchanted grove glimmered softly in the moonlight, the golden hues of its ancient oak casting a warm glow over Baby and Pip as they rested. The night seemed peaceful, with the gentle hum of the grove's magic surrounding them. Baby stretched out on the mossy ground, her tail thumping lazily as Pip fluttered down to perch on a nearby root.

"This place is incredible," Baby barked softly, her voice filled with wonder. "I've never seen anything like it."

Pip grinned, his small wings twitching. "Told you it's special. But don't get too comfortable, pup. The forest has its surprises, and not all of them are as friendly as me."

Just as Pip finished speaking, a distant, mournful howl echoed through the trees, slicing through the tranquility of the grove. Baby's ears perked up, her head snapping toward the sound. The howl was long and sorrowful, carrying a hint of desperation. It sent a chill down her spine, not because it was scary, but because it sounded so...lonely.

Pip flapped his wings nervously, his usual bravado faltering. "Uh, okay. That's new. And creepy. I don't usually hear howls like that around here."

Baby stood, her tail stiff, her sharp senses now on high alert. Her ears twitched, picking up faint rustling sounds and a second, shorter howl in the distance. "It's coming from deeper in the forest," she said, her nose twitching as she caught a faint scent on the breeze. "Something—or someone—is out there."

Pip hesitated, his eyes darting between Baby and the darkened woods beyond the grove. "You're not seriously thinking about investigating, are you? I mean, it could be dangerous! What if it's...you know, not friendly?"

Baby gave him a determined look, her tail wagging just slightly. "It sounds like whoever's out there needs help. I can't just ignore it."

Pip sighed, flapping his wings to lift off the root. "Alright, fine. But if we run into something scary, you're using those vampire powers to protect me, got it?"

Baby barked in agreement, already bounding toward the sound. Pip followed reluctantly, his small wings beating furiously to keep up.

As they ventured deeper into the forest, the trees grew denser, their branches twisting together like skeletal fingers. The air was cooler here, carrying the faint scent of damp earth and pine. Baby's heightened senses kicked into overdrive. Her sharp ears picked up every tiny sound—the skittering of a mouse, the rustle of leaves in the breeze, and, most importantly, the faint, irregular footsteps of something moving through the underbrush ahead.

She sniffed the air, catching a peculiar scent. It was earthy, like damp fur, but there was something else—a warmth that reminded her of the way Lucy smelled when she hugged Baby after a long day. It wasn't threatening; it was...familiar, somehow.

Another howl rang out, closer this time, and Baby quickened her pace. Pip zipped ahead, his small form darting between the trees. "Whoever it is, they're just up ahead," he called back.

They emerged into a small clearing, where the moonlight pierced through the canopy, casting silvery beams onto the forest floor. In the center of the clearing stood a small figure, its head tilted back as it let out another mournful howl. It was a puppy, covered in soft, shaggy fur the color of rich chestnut, with piercing golden eyes that glinted in the moonlight. Its oversized paws and slightly clumsy stance made it clear it was still very young.

Baby froze, her heart aching at the sight. The little pup looked scared and lost, its howls a plea for help. Before Baby could step forward, Pip whispered nervously, "Uh, Baby? That's not just any puppy. Look at its ears—and those claws."

Baby took a closer look. The pup's ears were pointed and tufted, its claws slightly curved and sharper than any ordinary dog's. As the pup turned toward them, Baby noticed its teeth—small but unmistakably sharp.

"It's a werewolf," Pip whispered, his voice shaking. "A baby werewolf."

Baby didn't hesitate. She trotted forward, her tail wagging in a friendly greeting. The werewolf pup flinched at first, its golden eyes wide with fear, but Baby stopped a few paces away and barked softly, lowering herself into a playful bow.

"It's okay," she said gently. "I'm not here to hurt you. My name's Baby. What's yours?"

The pup blinked, its ears twitching at Baby's warm tone. "I... I'm Max," it said hesitantly, its voice soft and trembling. "I got separated from my pack. I don't know how to get back."

Baby's heart swelled with sympathy. She stepped closer, nuzzling Max's side reassuringly. "Don't worry, Max. We'll help you find your way home."

Pip fluttered closer, still wary but softening as he saw Max's frightened expression. "Yeah, kid. We've got your back. But, uh, you don't have a big, scary werewolf parent nearby, do you? Because I don't do well with growling and snapping."

Max shook his head, his fur bristling slightly. "They were here earlier, but we got separated when some hunters came through the forest. I ran and hid, but now I'm lost."

Baby growled softly at the mention of hunters. "Don't worry, Max. We'll keep you safe. Do you remember which direction your pack was headed?"

Max sniffed the air, his nose twitching. "I think they went toward the big hollow tree near the creek. But I don't know how to get there from here."

Baby wagged her tail. "I do! I've been all over this forest. Follow me."

With Pip leading the way from above and Baby guiding Max on the ground, the trio made their way through the forest. Max quickly warmed up to Baby, his tail wagging as they walked. He even started to tell her about his pack—how his parents were the leaders, how he loved playing chase with his siblings, and how he had been too curious and wandered off when he heard the hunters.

As they neared the creek, Baby's sharp ears picked up faint howls in the distance. Max's ears perked up, and he howled back, his voice trembling but hopeful. The answering howls grew louder, and soon, a group of larger shadows emerged from the trees.

Max's pack had found him.

The reunion was joyous, with Max's parents nuzzling him protectively and his siblings bounding around him in excitement. One of the larger werewolves, presumably Max's mother, stepped forward and bowed her head to Baby and Pip.

"Thank you for bringing Max back to us," she said, her voice warm and full of gratitude. "We owe you a great debt."

Baby barked happily, her tail wagging. "I'm just glad he's safe."

As the werewolf pack disappeared back into the forest, Max paused and turned back to Baby and Pip. "Thank you," he said, his golden eyes shining. "I'll never forget this. If you ever need help, just howl. I'll hear you."

Baby watched as Max bounded after his family, her heart swelling with pride. As she and Pip made their way back toward the enchanted grove, Pip let out a low whistle.

"Well, that was something," he said, glancing at Baby. "You've got a knack for this whole hero thing, pup."

Baby grinned, her fangs glinting in the moonlight. "I just did what felt right. But you know what? I think we make a pretty great team."

Pip chuckled. "Yeah, yeah. Just don't expect me to handle all the scary stuff."

Together, they disappeared into the forest, ready for whatever adventure the night would bring next.

Chapter 4: Vampire Tricks and Puppy Treats

The annual Moonlit Hollow Pet Costume Parade was one of the town's most anticipated events, and this year, Baby couldn't wait to join the fun. The streets buzzed with excitement as townsfolk and their furry companions gathered in elaborate costumes, ready to strut down the cobblestone streets. Booths selling homemade pet treats, colorful collars, and costume accessories lined the square, filling the air with the scent of freshly baked goodies and a chorus of happy barks.

Lucy had spent days preparing Baby's costume—a glittery bat cape with little wings that flapped whenever Baby moved. It was a fitting choice, though it made Baby chuckle to herself; the townsfolk had no idea just how accurate the costume really was.

"Alright, Baby," Lucy said as she adjusted the tiny cape around Baby's shoulders. "You're going to steal the show. Just remember to behave, okay? No chasing cats or trying to snag treats off the judges' table."

Baby wagged her tail enthusiastically. She was ready for the parade, but she couldn't resist the idea of showing off her newfound agility. After all, how often did she get the chance to leap and bound in front of an audience? Pip, perched discreetly on a lamppost nearby, had warned her to be careful, but Baby couldn't help herself.

The parade kicked off with a burst of excitement. Dogs dressed as superheroes, pirates, and princesses trotted down the street, their owners proudly leading them by colorful leashes. Cats in regal robes lounged on floats, clearly unimpressed by the fanfare. Even a rabbit dressed as a tiny wizard hopped along in a carriage.

When it was Baby's turn, she strutted confidently onto the parade route, her bat wings fluttering as the crowd clapped and cheered. Lucy walked beside her, waving to the crowd. Baby soaked in the applause, her tail wagging furiously.

"Isn't she adorable?" one woman cooed. "Look at those little wings!"

"She's got the cutest costume!" another exclaimed.

Baby decided to take things up a notch. She darted ahead of Lucy, her paws barely touching the ground as she performed a series of graceful leaps. She bounded over a hay bale obstacle, landing effortlessly, and spun in a playful circle before leaping into the air and catching a falling autumn leaf in her mouth. The crowd erupted into applause.

"That's one talented pup!" someone shouted.

Baby barked proudly, basking in the attention. She caught sight of Pip on the lamppost, frantically gesturing for her to slow down. Ignoring him, Baby prepared for her grand finale—a high jump onto a decorative pumpkin stack. She crouched low, her muscles tensing, and sprang into the air. The crowd gasped as she soared higher than any ordinary dog could, landing perfectly on the topmost pumpkin.

But as Baby grinned triumphantly, disaster struck. The motion of her landing caused her fangs to slip from beneath her lips, glinting in the sunlight. A hush fell over the crowd.

"Did you see that?" someone whispered. "Her teeth—they're so sharp!"

"Are those part of the costume?" another person asked, leaning closer.

Baby's ears flattened in panic. She could feel the curious gazes of the crowd as more people began to notice. Lucy, too, had frozen, her eyes wide as she stared at Baby's exposed fangs.

Thinking quickly, Baby tilted her head and let out a playful bark, sticking out her tongue to cover her fangs. She bounded down from the pumpkin stack and wagged her tail, pretending as if nothing had happened. To further distract the crowd, she grabbed a prop broomstick from a nearby float and pranced around with it, earning a wave of laughter and applause.

"She's such a little show-off!" someone laughed.

"That's the best vampire dog costume I've ever seen!" another person called out.

Lucy quickly recovered, clapping her hands to draw attention away from Baby's teeth. "Alright, let's hear it for Baby, the flying bat-dog!" she said, her voice cheerful but slightly strained. The crowd cheered, and Baby let out a relieved bark, trotting back to Lucy's side.

As the parade continued, Lucy leaned down and whispered, "That was a close one, Baby. You've got to be more careful." Baby wagged her tail apologetically, nudging Lucy's leg in a silent promise to behave—at least for the rest of the parade.

After the event, Baby and Lucy visited the booths in the square. Lucy picked up a bag of pumpkin-flavored dog treats for Baby, who sniffed them eagerly. Pip, who had flown down to join them, perched on a nearby table, shaking his head.

"You're lucky they thought it was part of your costume," Pip said, his voice low. "Next time, keep those fangs tucked in, pup. You almost gave away the whole secret."

Baby barked softly, giving Pip a playful nudge with her nose. "Relax, Pip. I handled it."

"You call that handling it?" Pip muttered. "You're lucky humans are so quick to explain things away. 'Oh, it's just part of the costume.' Hah! If they knew the truth..."

Baby didn't let Pip's scolding dampen her spirits. She had learned her lesson—sort of. The day had been exhilarating, and despite the near-disaster, she couldn't help but feel proud of her performance.

As the sun set over Moonlit Hollow, Baby, Lucy, and Pip made their way home, the town square glowing with strings of lanterns and the laughter of happy parade-goers. Baby curled up on her blanket by the fireplace that evening, her belly full of treats and her heart full of pride.

Sure, she'd made a small mistake, but she had also dazzled the crowd and made Lucy proud. And if anyone had noticed her fangs, they'd chalked it up to her "vampire costume." Baby closed her eyes, already dreaming of her next adventure—and how she'd use her powers a little more carefully next time.

Chapter 5: The Glow-in-the-Dark Collar

The first hint of twilight painted the sky in hues of orange and purple as Lucy rummaged through a small parcel on the kitchen table. Baby watched her with curious eyes, her head tilted to one side. The package had arrived earlier that day, wrapped in brown paper and tied with a simple twine bow. Baby could tell it was something special; Lucy had been unusually excited when she opened it.

"Here it is!" Lucy exclaimed, pulling out a small object and holding it up for Baby to see. It was a collar—sleek, midnight black with tiny silver accents that sparkled as they caught the light. At the center of the collar hung a delicate charm shaped like a crescent moon, its surface engraved with intricate designs.

"This," Lucy said, kneeling to fasten the collar around Baby's neck, "is your new glow-in-the-dark collar. It'll help me keep an eye on you during our evening walks—and during whatever mischief you get up to at night."

Baby wagged her tail as Lucy secured the collar. It fit snugly but comfortably, and as Lucy stepped back to admire her handiwork, Baby felt a subtle warmth radiate from the charm. She sniffed at it curiously, noticing a faint, magical hum she couldn't quite place.

"Let's test it out!" Lucy said, switching off the lights in the kitchen. The collar immediately came to life, emitting a soft, silvery glow that bathed Baby in an ethereal light. The crescent moon charm seemed to shimmer even brighter, casting tiny beams of light that danced across the walls.

Baby barked in delight, prancing around the kitchen to see the glow follow her every move. Lucy laughed, clapping her hands. "It's perfect! Now I'll always know where you are, even in the dark."

That evening, Baby couldn't wait to test her new collar during a nighttime adventure. As soon as Lucy was asleep, Baby crept out of the house, her paws making no sound on the wooden floor. The collar's soft glow illuminated her path as she trotted toward the edge of town, where the forest began. Pip was waiting for her, hanging upside down from a low tree branch.

"Well, look at you, all fancy and glowing," Pip teased, fluttering down to inspect the collar more closely. "What's the occasion?"

"Lucy gave it to me," Baby said, puffing out her chest proudly. "She wants me to stay safe at night."

Pip nodded approvingly. "Not a bad idea. It's pretty handy—and stylish, too. But...do you feel that?" He squinted at the crescent moon charm, his small nose twitching. "There's something...different about it."

Baby tilted her head. "Different how?"

Pip flapped his wings, hovering closer. "I don't know. It's faint, but there's definitely magic in there. You might want to be careful with that thing."

Baby wagged her tail, dismissing his concerns. "It's just a collar, Pip. Let's go explore!"

The two ventured deeper into the forest, the collar's glow lighting their way. Baby marveled at how much easier it was to navigate the dark paths with the soft light guiding her. The usual shadows that danced under the moonlight seemed less intimidating, and every rustling leaf and distant sound felt more like part of an adventure than a threat.

As they reached the enchanted grove, Baby suddenly felt a strange sensation. The crescent moon charm grew warmer against her chest, and the light from the collar began to pulse rhythmically, like a heartbeat. Baby stopped in her tracks, her ears perking up.

"Pip," she said, her voice low. "Something's happening."

Before Pip could respond, the grove seemed to come alive. The ancient oak tree at the grove's center shimmered faintly, its golden light brightening as if in response to the collar's glow. The air around them filled with a soft hum, and Baby felt an invisible force tugging at her collar, urging her toward the tree.

"Okay, that's definitely magic," Pip muttered, flitting nervously to Baby's side. "What did I say about being careful?"

Baby ignored him, drawn forward by the collar's gentle pull. As she approached the oak tree, the crescent moon charm emitted a bright, silvery flash, and a swirling pattern of light appeared on the ground at Baby's paws. The pattern resembled ancient runes, their shapes shifting and glowing like living beings.

"Whoa," Pip whispered, his eyes wide. "This is...something else."

The light grew brighter, and suddenly, Baby felt a surge of energy coursing through her. It was unlike anything she'd ever experienced before—a mix of warmth and power that made her feel invincible. Her senses sharpened even further, her vision piercing through the shadows with perfect clarity. She could hear the tiniest movements, like the flutter of a moth's wings, and her paws tingled with an energy that made her want to leap higher and run faster than ever.

"Baby," Pip said cautiously, "I think that collar just unlocked some kind of...hidden power."

Baby looked down at the glowing runes, then back at the collar. She barked softly, a mix of awe and excitement. "I don't know what this is, but it feels amazing!"

As the light began to fade, the runes on the ground disappeared, and the grove returned to its usual, tranquil state. The collar's glow dimmed slightly, but Baby could still feel the lingering energy within her. She turned to Pip, her tail wagging.

"Let's see what I can do now!"

Over the next hour, Baby tested her newfound abilities. Her agility had increased tenfold; she could leap from one branch to another with ease, her paws barely grazing the ground. Her speed was incredible, allowing her to dash across the grove in the blink of an eye. And her strength surprised even her—she managed to push aside a fallen log that had been blocking a path, something she wouldn't have been able to do before.

Pip watched in amazement, though his expression remained cautious. "Okay, you're officially the coolest vampire-dog I've ever met. But you've got to keep this under wraps, Baby. If anyone finds out about this collar, they're going to want it—and not for good reasons."

Baby nodded, her excitement tempered by Pip's warning. "You're right. I'll be careful. But this collar—it's more than just a gift from Lucy. It's connected to this forest, to the magic here. I think it's meant for something bigger."

Pip sighed, folding his wings. "Fine, but no crazy stunts, okay? The last thing we need is you turning into a superhero and drawing attention."

Baby barked playfully, nudging Pip with her nose. "No promises."

As the first rays of dawn began to peek over the horizon, Baby and Pip made their way back to Moonlit Hollow. The collar's glow had dimmed completely, leaving it looking like any ordinary accessory. But Baby knew it was far from ordinary. It was a key to something extraordinary, and she couldn't wait to discover what other secrets it might unlock.

Chapter 6: The Moonlight Chase

The moon hung high over Moonlit Hollow, casting its silvery light across the quiet town. The streets were empty, the cobblestones glistening faintly under the glow. Most of the townsfolk were tucked in their beds, dreaming of the next day's events. But Baby was wide awake, her vampire instincts fully alive in the stillness of the night.

She trotted along the edge of the forest, her glow-in-the-dark collar faintly illuminating her path. Pip flew beside her, his tiny wings making soft whooshing sounds as he glided through the air.

"I'm telling you, Pip, there's something magical about tonight," Baby said, sniffing the air. The night carried an unusual crispness, and the moon seemed brighter than usual, its light almost tangible.

"You say that every night," Pip teased, rolling his eyes. "But fine, let's see what kind of trouble you can get us into this time."

As they neared the town square, a soft, ethereal glow caught Baby's attention. A small ball of light floated just above the cobblestones, its silvery luminescence flickering like a firefly. Baby froze, her ears perking up.

"What's that?" she asked, her tail wagging in curiosity.

Pip squinted at the glowing orb. "It's...moonlight? But it's moving."

Before Pip could stop her, Baby bounded forward, her excitement getting the better of her. The glowing ball darted away, skimming just above the ground. Baby let out a playful bark and took off after it, her paws barely touching the cobblestones.

"Baby, wait!" Pip shouted, flapping furiously to keep up. "That thing could be dangerous!"

Baby didn't hear him—or if she did, she ignored him. The ball of moonlight danced and twirled, weaving between lampposts and flower pots. It seemed almost alive, as though it were teasing her, daring her to catch it. Baby leaped over a wooden bench, her glowing collar lighting her way as she pursued the mysterious orb through the empty streets.

The chase led her past the bakery, where the scent of day-old pastries lingered in the air, and down the narrow alley by the town library. The glowing ball zipped through the town with surprising speed, but Baby was determined to catch it. She pushed herself faster, her vampire agility kicking in as she leaped over obstacles and rounded sharp corners.

Finally, the ball of moonlight darted into the garden of the mayor's house, where the town's grumpiest feline, Mr. Whiskers, was known to reside. Baby hesitated for the briefest moment, her instincts telling her this might not be the best idea. But the thrill of the chase was too much to resist. With a quick glance back at Pip, who was still shouting warnings, Baby bounded into the garden.

The ball of light hovered just above a neatly trimmed hedge, flickering mischievously. Baby crouched low, her muscles tensing as she prepared to pounce. With a powerful leap, she launched herself into the air, her paws outstretched.

At that exact moment, a loud, irritated yowl pierced the quiet night. Baby landed not on the glowing ball, but on the garden's stone path, skidding to a stop just inches away from a very startled—and very angry—Mr. Whiskers.

The old cat's fur bristled as he arched his back, his green eyes narrowing into slits. He let out another yowl, this one loud enough to wake the mayor, and swatted at Baby with his sharp claws.

"Uh-oh," Baby muttered, backing away quickly. "Sorry, Mr. Whiskers! Didn't mean to wake you!"

Mr. Whiskers was having none of it. He hissed loudly, his tail lashing as he advanced on Baby. The ball of moonlight, apparently amused by the chaos, flickered brightly and darted away, leaving Baby to deal with the consequences of her playful misstep.

Pip landed on a nearby fence post, shaking his head. "I told you this was a bad idea. Now look what you've done!"

Baby dodged another swipe from Mr. Whiskers and bolted toward the garden gate, her tail tucked between her legs. The old cat chased after her, his yowls growing louder with each step. Baby leaped over the gate with ease, landing gracefully on the other side. Mr. Whiskers stopped at the gate, glaring at her with a look that promised he wouldn't forget this slight anytime soon.

Unfortunately, the commotion didn't go unnoticed. The lights in the mayor's house flicked on, and a window creaked open. "What's all this racket?" came the mayor's gruff voice. "Whiskers, what's going on out there?"

Baby ducked behind a bush, her glowing collar dimming as she tried to stay hidden. Pip fluttered down to join her, his tiny wings twitching nervously.

"You're glowing like a lantern, Baby," Pip whispered. "He's going to see you!"

Thinking quickly, Baby pressed her nose to the crescent moon charm on her collar. To her relief, the glow faded completely, leaving her hidden in the shadows. She held her breath as the mayor peered out the window, his bushy eyebrows furrowed.

"Must've been those pesky raccoons again," the mayor grumbled before shutting the window. The lights in the house flickered off, and silence returned to the garden.

Baby exhaled in relief, her tail wagging weakly. "That was close."

Pip gave her an exasperated look. "Close? You almost woke up the entire town! And what was that thing, anyway? A glowing ball of moonlight? What kind of magic are we dealing with here?"

Baby shrugged, her playful spirit undimmed. "I don't know, but it was fun! And now we know my collar can dim its light when I need it to."

Pip sighed, shaking his head. "You're lucky you're cute, pup. Let's get out of here before Mr. Whiskers decides to come back for round two."

As they made their way back to the forest, Baby couldn't help but grin. The moonlight chase had been exhilarating, even if it had ended with a grumpy cat and a close call. She glanced at her collar, the crescent moon charm now glowing faintly once more. It seemed to hum softly, as though it were pleased with her antics.

Baby knew she'd have to be more careful in the future—at least when it came to waking up cranky cats and their even crankier owners. But she also knew one thing for certain: the nights in Moonlit Hollow were full of surprises, and she was ready for whatever adventure came next.

Chapter 7: Baby Saves the Day

The night began with an eerie stillness in Moonlit Hollow. The usual chirping of crickets and rustling leaves seemed to hold their breath as thick clouds rolled in, veiling the moonlight. The air felt heavy, charged with the kind of electricity that heralded a storm. Inside Lucy's cozy cottage, Baby curled up on her blanket by the hearth, her glowing collar casting soft patterns on the walls as Lucy read a book nearby.

Suddenly, a sharp crack of thunder shattered the silence, followed by a brilliant flash of lightning that lit up the entire town. Baby's ears perked up, and she let out a low bark of concern. Lucy set her book down, her brow furrowing as she glanced toward the window.

"That's quite the storm brewing," she said, her voice calm but tinged with worry. "I'd better check the emergency candles and flashlight, just in case."

As Lucy rummaged through a drawer, the lights flickered once, twice, and then went out completely, plunging the cottage into darkness. Baby barked again, her glowing collar now the only source of light in the room.

"Well, that answers that," Lucy muttered. "Looks like the whole street's out." She lit a candle, the flame casting flickering shadows, and knelt beside Baby. "At least we've got your collar to help us see."

Baby wagged her tail, sensing Lucy's unease. The storm outside intensified, rain pounding against the windows and wind howling through the trees. Another loud crack of thunder made the floorboards tremble. Lucy stood and peeked out the window, her face tightening as she saw the dim outlines of her neighbors gathering on the street.

"I should check on everyone," she said, grabbing her raincoat. "Come on, Baby. We might need your help tonight."

Outside, the storm was even more intense. The rain fell in sheets, soaking the cobblestones and creating puddles that reflected the occasional flash of lightning. Baby stayed close to Lucy, her glowing collar cutting through the darkness like a beacon. As they reached the street, several of their neighbors waved them over, their faces lit by the weak glow of lanterns and cell phone screens.

"It's the whole town," said Mrs. Whiskerbee, clutching an umbrella that was threatening to turn inside out. "The power's out everywhere, and the storm's knocked down some trees."

"And one of those trees blocked the bridge out of town," added Mr. Jacobs, who ran the general store. "The road's flooded, and we've got a few folks stuck on the other side."

Lucy frowned, glancing down at Baby. "If the bridge is blocked, we'll need to find another way to help them. Baby, think you can guide us?"

Baby barked confidently, wagging her tail. She could feel the faint hum of her collar's magic, as if it were responding to the urgency of the moment. Lucy smiled and turned back to the neighbors.

"Alright, let's form a group and check on everyone. Baby's collar will light the way."

Leading the group, Baby padded ahead, her collar casting a silvery glow that cut through the sheets of rain. She relied on her heightened senses, her sharp ears picking up distant voices and her nose detecting faint traces of human scent. The group followed her closely, their steps careful on the slick cobblestones.

As they neared the edge of town, Baby stopped abruptly, her ears swiveling toward a faint sound. Over the howling wind and pounding rain, she heard what sounded like muffled cries. She barked and dashed forward, leading Lucy and the others to a small alley between two buildings.

There, huddled under an overhang, was a family with two young children, their faces pale and wet from the rain.

"Thank goodness you found us!" the mother exclaimed as Lucy hurried to help them. "We were trying to make it to the community center, but we got lost in the dark."

"You're safe now," Lucy assured her, handing over her umbrella. "Follow us; we'll guide you there."

Baby stayed close to the family, her glowing collar illuminating the path as they rejoined the rest of the group. Together, they made their way to the community center, a sturdy brick building that served as a shelter during emergencies.

Inside the community center, the air was warm and bustling with activity. Volunteers handed out blankets and hot drinks, and lanterns provided a soft, flickering light. Baby shook the rain from her coat and looked up at Lucy, who smiled down at her.

"You're doing great, Baby," Lucy said, giving her a scratch behind the ears. "But we're not done yet. We still need to help those folks on the other side of the bridge."

Just then, the mayor approached, his expression grim. "Lucy, I hear you've been helping out," he said, glancing at Baby. "We've got a few people stuck across the bridge. The water's rising fast, and we need to get to them before it's too late."

"I think Baby can help," Lucy said. "She's been leading us through the storm all night."

The mayor nodded. "If she's up for it, let's move quickly."

With the mayor and a few other volunteers in tow, Baby led the way toward the flooded bridge. The water rushed dangerously fast, and a large tree trunk blocked the only safe crossing. Baby sniffed the air, her glowing collar reflecting off the turbulent water. She heard faint shouts from the other side and barked to alert the group.

"We'll need to find another way across," the mayor said, scanning the area.

Baby's sharp eyes caught a narrow path through the trees, one that seemed to lead to a shallow part of the creek. She barked and darted toward it, her collar lighting the way. The group followed her, stepping carefully over roots and rocks. The shallow crossing was slippery but manageable, and soon they reached the stranded group on the other side.

The stranded townsfolk cheered as Baby arrived, her glowing collar a welcome sight in the darkness. With the volunteers' help, they crossed back safely, guided every step of the way by Baby's light.

By the time they returned to the community center, the storm had begun to subside. The rain lessened to a gentle drizzle, and the wind grew calmer. Inside, the townsfolk gathered around Baby, showering her with praise and gratitude.

"You're a hero, Baby!" Mrs. Whiskerbee said, offering her a treat from her pocket.

The mayor knelt down and gave Baby a rare smile. "You saved the day, little one. Moonlit Hollow owes you."

Baby wagged her tail happily, her chest swelling with pride. She looked up at Lucy, who beamed with pride and knelt to hug her tightly.

"You're incredible, Baby," Lucy whispered. "I don't know what I'd do without you."

As the sun began to rise, casting warm light over the wet streets, the power in Moonlit Hollow flickered back on. Baby, exhausted but content, curled up on her blanket by the hearth, her collar now glowing faintly. She had faced the storm, guided her town to safety, and discovered just how much her courage and quick thinking could accomplish.

Even as she drifted off to sleep, Baby knew one thing for certain: Moonlit Hollow was her home, and she would always be ready to protect it—no matter what the night brought.

Chapter 8: A New Friendship

The sun had barely dipped below the horizon, casting a soft twilight glow over Moonlit Hollow, when Baby decided to explore the forest near the enchanted grove. After her heroic adventure during the storm, she felt more confident than ever, her tail wagging with excitement as she padded along the well-trodden path. Pip flitted beside her, occasionally darting ahead to scout for anything interesting.

"You're in an unusually good mood," Pip remarked, glancing at Baby as he landed on a low-hanging branch. "Looking for something specific, or just restless?"

Baby barked playfully, her collar glowing faintly as it began to catch the moonlight. "I just feel like tonight might be special. Don't you ever get that feeling, Pip? Like something unexpected is about to happen?"

"Unexpected usually means trouble," Pip muttered, but his wings twitched with curiosity. "Lead the way, pup. Let's see what kind of chaos we stumble into this time."

As they ventured deeper into the forest, the soft rustle of leaves and distant hoot of an owl created a peaceful backdrop. The grove's golden light shimmered faintly in the distance, but Baby's sharp ears picked up a different sound—a faint, high-pitched squeak. She stopped, her ears swiveling as she tried to pinpoint its location.

"Did you hear that?" she asked, her voice hushed.

Pip landed on her head, peering into the shadows. "Hear what? All I hear is your heavy breathing."

Baby ignored him, focusing on the sound. It came again, this time a little louder—a soft, trembling whimper that made her heart ache. Without a word, she darted toward the source, her glowing collar lighting the way.

Baby stopped near a hollow log nestled under the roots of a large oak tree. The whimpering grew louder as she approached. Lowering her head, she peeked into the log and saw a small, quivering ball of spines—clearly a hedgehog, though its tiny body was curled so tightly it was impossible to see its face.

"Hey there," Baby said gently, wagging her tail. "It's okay. I won't hurt you."

The hedgehog trembled even more, pressing itself deeper into the log. Its voice, small and shaky, responded, "P-please go away. I d-don't want any trouble."

Baby's heart melted at the sound. She lay down on the ground, her head resting on her paws, trying to appear as non-threatening as possible. "I'm not here to cause trouble. My name's Baby. What's yours?"

After a long pause, the hedgehog uncurled just enough to reveal a pair of wide, nervous eyes. "I'm Thorn," he said, his voice barely above a whisper.

"That's a great name," Baby said warmly. "What are you doing out here all by yourself, Thorn?"

Thorn hesitated, glancing around nervously. "I got separated from my family. We were moving to a new burrow when the storm hit, and I...I got scared and hid. When I came out, they were gone."

Baby's tail drooped, her heart aching for the little hedgehog. "That must've been so scary. But you're not alone anymore, Thorn. I'll help you find your family."

Thorn shook his head quickly, his spines bristling. "No, I can't! What if I get lost again? Or what if something scary finds me?"

Baby thought for a moment, then smiled. "You're not going to be alone this time. I'll be with you, and so will Pip. Right, Pip?"

Pip, who had been watching from a nearby branch, sighed dramatically. "Sure, why not? Let's add 'hedgehog babysitter' to my résumé."

Thorn glanced between them, his fear slowly giving way to curiosity. "You'd...really help me?"

"Of course!" Baby said, her voice bright and reassuring. "Friends help each other, and I think we're going to be great friends."

Over the next hour, Baby and Pip worked to coax Thorn out of his hiding spot. Baby encouraged him with her playful antics, while Pip shared stories of his adventures in the forest. Slowly but surely, Thorn began to relax, his tiny legs unfolding as he crept out of the log.

"There you go!" Baby said, wagging her tail. "See? It's not so bad out here."

Thorn managed a small smile. "I guess it's...not as scary with you around."

The trio set off to search for Thorn's family, Baby leading the way with her glowing collar lighting the path. Thorn stayed close to her side, his tiny legs moving quickly to keep up. Pip flew just above them, keeping an eye out for any signs of other hedgehogs.

As they walked, Baby talked to Thorn, asking him about his favorite foods and places he'd visited. She learned that Thorn loved fresh berries and had always dreamed of seeing the enchanted grove but had been too afraid to venture into the deeper parts of the forest.

"You'll love the grove," Baby said, her excitement infectious. "It's magical—just like you."

Thorn blushed, his spines bristling slightly. "I don't think I'm magical. I'm just...me."

"You're braver than you think," Baby replied. "You came out of that log, didn't you? And now you're exploring the forest with us. That's pretty magical if you ask me."

As dawn began to break, the trio reached a small clearing where the scent of hedgehogs lingered strongly in the air. Thorn's ears perked up, and he squeaked in excitement. "That's them! That's my family!"

Sure enough, a group of hedgehogs emerged from a cluster of bushes, their tiny faces lighting up when they saw Thorn. His mother rushed forward, nuzzling him with obvious relief.

"Thorn, we've been so worried!" she exclaimed. "Where have you been?"

"I got lost during the storm," Thorn admitted, glancing at Baby. "But Baby and Pip helped me find my way back."

The hedgehog family turned to Baby and Pip, their eyes full of gratitude. "Thank you," Thorn's mother said. "We're forever in your debt."

Baby barked happily. "No need to thank me. I'm just glad Thorn's safe."

As the hedgehogs disappeared into the underbrush, Thorn turned back one last time. "Thank you, Baby. For everything. I hope we can see each other again soon."

"Anytime," Baby replied, her tail wagging. "You're my friend now, Thorn. And friends always find their way back to each other."

As Baby and Pip made their way back toward Moonlit Hollow, Pip gave her a sideways glance. "You're pretty good at this whole 'hero' thing, you know that?"

Baby grinned, her collar glowing faintly in the early morning light. "I just like helping people—and making new friends."

Pip rolled his eyes but couldn't hide his smile. "Well, if you keep this up, Moonlit Hollow might just have to throw you a parade."

Baby laughed, her heart full as they trotted home. Thorn's bravery and their newfound friendship reminded her that even the smallest creatures could have the biggest hearts—and that kindness could light up the darkest nights.

Chapter 9: The Shadowy Stranger

The forest surrounding Moonlit Hollow always held an air of mystery, but tonight, it seemed different. The usual soft hum of magic that Baby had come to know felt heavier, tinged with something unknown. A faint breeze rustled the trees, carrying whispers that made the leaves quiver and Pip's wings twitch nervously.

Baby trotted cautiously through the woods, her glowing collar dimmed to avoid drawing too much attention. Pip flew beside her, his usual playful chatter replaced with silence as he scanned the shadows.

"I don't like this," Pip muttered, his voice low. "Something's out there. I can feel it."

Baby sniffed the air, her sharp senses on high alert. "I know. It feels...different tonight. Not bad, just...unfamiliar."

The two paused at the edge of a clearing. The moonlight pierced through the canopy, casting eerie patterns on the ground. Baby's ears twitched as she caught the faintest sound—a shuffle, soft and deliberate, coming from the other side of the clearing.

"Did you hear that?" she whispered.

"Of course I heard it," Pip replied, his tiny claws gripping a low branch. "We should go back. Whatever it is, it's not our problem."

Baby shook her head. "If something's lurking in the forest, it *is* our problem. We can't just ignore it."

Before Pip could argue further, a shadow moved at the edge of the clearing. It was tall and indistinct, blending almost seamlessly with the darkness. Baby's heart raced, but she stood her ground, her glowing collar brightening slightly as if to push back the encroaching shadows.

"Who's there?" she called, her voice firm but not aggressive.

The shadow didn't respond, instead retreating deeper into the forest. Baby took a cautious step forward, but Pip flapped in front of her face.

"Whoa, whoa, whoa! You're seriously going after that thing? Have you lost your mind?"

Baby nudged him aside gently. "We can't just let it roam around. What if it's dangerous?"

Pip groaned but followed as Baby moved toward the shadow's path. The trail led deeper into the woods, where the trees grew thicker and the air cooler. The faint sound of running water hinted at the nearby creek, but another sound soon drowned it out—a soft, rhythmic padding of paws.

"Max!" Baby barked softly as the werewolf pup emerged from the shadows, his golden eyes wide and alert.

"Baby! Pip!" Max exclaimed, his tail wagging slightly despite the tension in the air. "I've been tracking something weird. It's big, and it moves really quietly. I thought it might be trouble, so I came to find you."

Baby smiled, reassured by the pup's presence. "We're on the same trail. Let's stick together."

The trio followed the shadowy figure's path until they reached an ancient part of the forest that even Baby hadn't explored. The trees here were massive, their gnarled roots twisting like the fingers of giants. The air felt thick with magic, each step tingling with energy.

Suddenly, a loud *hoot* broke the silence, deep and resonant. Baby froze, her ears swiveling toward the sound. High above them, perched on a thick branch, was an enormous owl. Its feathers were a mix of silver and midnight blue, shimmering faintly in the moonlight. Its golden eyes glowed with an otherworldly light, and its gaze fixed on the trio below.

"Well, well," the owl said, its voice deep and smooth. "What have we here? A vampire pup, a mischievous bat, and a young werewolf. Quite the unlikely team."

"Who are you?" Baby asked, her tail stiff but not threatening. "Were you the one we saw in the clearing?"

The owl ruffled its feathers, its talons gripping the branch tightly. "I am Eldrin, the Keeper of Riddles. I've been watching you, little one. Your bravery and curiosity have drawn my attention."

Pip groaned, folding his wings. "Oh great, a magical owl with a penchant for riddles. Can we just skip to the part where you tell us what you want?"

Eldrin tilted his head, his glowing eyes narrowing. "Patience, little bat. You three have stumbled into my domain, and as such, you must prove your worth before I share my wisdom."

Max stepped forward, his ears perked. "Prove our worth? How?"

Eldrin's beak curved into what could only be described as an amused smirk. "By solving my riddle, of course. If you succeed, I will grant you knowledge that may aid you in your future endeavors. Fail, and you must leave my domain immediately."

Baby exchanged a glance with Pip and Max. "We're ready," she said confidently. "What's the riddle?"

Eldrin spread his wings, his voice echoing like a distant storm.

"I am not alive, yet I grow.

I do not have lungs, yet I need air.

I do not have a mouth, and yet I drown.

What am I?"

The forest fell silent as the trio pondered the riddle. Pip flitted nervously, muttering to himself. "Not alive, yet it grows? Doesn't have lungs but needs air? What kind of nonsense..."

Max frowned, his claws digging into the earth. "It's something natural, I think. But what?"

Baby sat quietly, her sharp mind turning the riddle over. "Not alive...yet it grows..." she murmured. Her glowing collar pulsed faintly, and inspiration struck. "Fire!" she exclaimed, her eyes bright. "It's fire! Fire isn't alive, but it grows when it's fed. It needs air to burn, and it's extinguished—drowned—by water."

Eldrin let out a low, approving hoot. "Well done, little one. You are correct."

The owl descended gracefully, landing on the forest floor. He looked at Baby with newfound respect. "You have proven yourselves worthy. As promised, I will share my wisdom."

Eldrin gestured with one massive wing, and a soft glow emanated from the ground. A map of the forest appeared, etched in light. "This is the ancient map of Moonlit Hollow's forest. It shows paths both seen and unseen, as well as places of great magic and danger. Use it wisely."

Baby stepped forward, her eyes wide with awe. "Thank you, Eldrin. We'll make sure to use it for good."

Eldrin nodded, his feathers shimmering. "I believe you will. Remember, the forest holds many secrets, but also great allies. Trust in each other, and you will overcome any challenge."

With that, Eldrin flapped his wings and soared into the night, disappearing into the shadows. The glowing map faded, but not before imprinting itself in Baby's memory.

As they made their way back to Moonlit Hollow, Pip broke the silence. "Well, that was...unexpected. I guess riddles aren't so bad when you have a smart pup like Baby around."

Max grinned, his tail wagging. "That was amazing, Baby. You're like a real hero."

Baby smiled, her glowing collar lighting their path. "We did it together. And now we have a map that can help us explore even more of the forest."

As the first rays of dawn peeked through the trees, Baby felt a sense of accomplishment. The shadowy stranger had turned out to be a wise ally, and she knew that with friends like Pip and Max by her side, there was no mystery they couldn't solve.

Chapter 10: The Harvest Festival

Moonlit Hollow's annual Harvest Festival was the highlight of the autumn season, a week-long celebration of abundance, community, and fun. The town square had been transformed into a wonderland of twinkling lights, colorful bunting, and the rich scents of baked goods, spiced cider, and roasted chestnuts. Stalls lined the cobblestone streets, selling everything from handcrafted trinkets to jars of golden honey and fresh apple pies. Children laughed as they bobbed for apples, and musicians played cheerful folk tunes that made everyone's spirits soar.

Baby trotted beside Lucy, her tail wagging excitedly as she took in the sights and smells. She wore a festive orange bandana tied around her neck, her glowing collar dimmed to blend in with the festive atmosphere. Pip flitted nearby, sticking close to the shadows to avoid drawing attention, though he couldn't resist sneaking a peek at the food stalls.

"This is amazing!" Baby barked, her nose twitching at the smell of pumpkin pies cooling on a nearby table. "There's so much to see—and eat!"

Lucy chuckled, bending down to scratch behind Baby's ears. "The Harvest Festival is my favorite time of year. I thought you'd enjoy it too."

Baby barked happily, her tail wagging even faster. As they wandered through the festival, Lucy stopped to chat with neighbors, leaving Baby free to explore. Pip landed on a fence post, his beady eyes scanning the bustling square.

"So, what's the plan, pup?" Pip asked. "Just sniffing around, or are you looking for something specific?"

Before Baby could answer, an announcement boomed from the center of the square. "Ladies and gentlemen, boys and girls, and all our furry friends, the annual **Harvest Pie-Eating Contest** is about to begin! Contestants, please make your way to the main tent!"

Baby's ears perked up, and her eyes sparkled with excitement. "Did you hear that, Pip? A pie-eating contest! I *have* to enter."

Pip groaned, shaking his head. "Seriously? You know those contests are for fun, right? No supernatural speed allowed."

Baby grinned mischievously. "Who says I can't have fun *and* win? Besides, I'll be careful. No one will notice."

Pip sighed, knowing there was no stopping her. "Fine, but if you get caught, I'm not helping you explain how a Boston Terrier can eat that fast."

The pie-eating contest was held under a large, striped tent, where long tables were set up with rows of pumpkin, apple, and berry pies. The smell alone was enough to make Baby's mouth water. Lucy guided her to the sign-up area, where other contestants—mostly larger dogs—were already lining up. Baby wagged her tail confidently, her eyes sparkling with determination.

"You sure about this, Baby?" Lucy asked, crouching to adjust her bandana. "Some of these dogs are pretty big."

Baby barked enthusiastically, letting Lucy know she was more than ready.

The contestants took their places, each dog seated in front of a fresh, steaming pie. A small crowd gathered around the tent, cheering for their favorite pets. The judge, Mr. Jacobs from the general store, stepped forward with a whistle in hand.

"Alright, everyone! The rules are simple: first dog to finish their pie wins. No paws allowed—just noses and mouths! On your marks...get set...go!"

The whistle blew, and chaos erupted as the dogs dove into their pies. Baby, however, had a plan. She darted forward, burying her face in the pie and using her vampire-enhanced speed to take tiny, rapid bites that were almost imperceptible to the onlookers. To everyone else, it looked like she was eating at a normal pace, but in reality, the pie was disappearing at lightning speed.

Beside her, a Golden Retriever named Duke was making steady progress, his large tongue scooping up chunks of pumpkin filling. On her other side, a scrappy terrier named Scout was licking furiously, his nose dusted with powdered sugar. Baby kept her focus, ensuring her movements stayed smooth and natural.

Lucy watched from the sidelines, her hands clasped nervously. "Come on, Baby," she whispered, though she couldn't help but smile at her dog's enthusiasm.

The crowd cheered louder as the contestants neared the end of their pies. Duke was slowing down, his enthusiasm waning as the richness of the pie took its toll. Scout was still determined, but the crust was proving difficult for him to manage. Baby, on the other hand, saw her opportunity. With one final burst of speed, she cleaned her plate, sitting back proudly and wagging her tail just as the judge blew the whistle.

"We have a winner!" Mr. Jacobs declared, lifting Baby's paw into the air. "Baby the Boston Terrier takes the prize!"

The crowd erupted into applause, and Lucy rushed forward to give Baby a big hug. "You did it, Baby! I'm so proud of you!"

Pip, watching from the shadows, shook his head with a mixture of exasperation and admiration. "You're lucky you're adorable, pup. No one suspects a thing."

As her prize, Baby received a golden medal shaped like a pumpkin and a basket of treats, including a small pie just for her. She carried the basket proudly as she and Lucy continued exploring the festival. Everywhere they went, people stopped to congratulate her, and Baby soaked up the attention with a wagging tail and a happy bark.

Later that evening, as the festival wound down and the lanterns cast a warm glow over the square, Baby and Lucy sat on a hay bale, sharing the small pie from her prize basket. Pip joined them, nibbling on a crumb Baby had saved for him.

"That was the most fun I've had in ages," Baby said, licking the last bit of filling from her nose.

"You know," Pip said, his voice light, "for a vampire dog, you're pretty good at blending in. Maybe too good."

Baby grinned, her collar glowing softly in the twilight. "That's the best part, Pip. I can be a little bit of everything—fast, clever, and kind. And as long as I'm having fun, that's all that matters."

Lucy leaned down, kissing the top of Baby's head. "You're one special pup, Baby. This town wouldn't be the same without you."

As the last of the festival-goers packed up and the music faded into the cool night air, Baby felt a warm sense of belonging. Moonlit Hollow was her home, and whether she was solving riddles, chasing moonlight, or winning pie-eating contests, she knew she'd always be surrounded by love and adventure.

Chapter 11: The Magic of Friendship

The enchanted forest surrounding Moonlit Hollow had always been a source of wonder and mystery. Its golden grove, shimmering trees, and magical creatures made it a sanctuary for the extraordinary. But one crisp autumn evening, as Baby and Pip strolled through its familiar paths, something felt off.

The hum of the forest, usually alive with magical energy, was subdued. The golden light of the enchanted grove was dimmer than usual, its vibrant glow replaced by a faint, flickering pulse. The air carried a weight that made Baby's fur bristle.

"Something's wrong," Baby murmured, her glowing collar faintly illuminating the path ahead.

Pip perched on her head, his wings twitching nervously. "You're telling me. It's too quiet, and not in the good, peaceful way."

As they reached the grove, Baby stopped, her sharp eyes scanning the area. The ancient oak tree at the center of the grove, once a beacon of magic, looked withered. Its golden vines drooped lifelessly, and the usual sparkle in its bark had faded to a dull gray. Baby's heart sank.

"We need to figure out what's happening," she said firmly. "The forest is in trouble."

The first step was gathering her friends. Baby and Pip quickly found Max at the edge of the forest, the young werewolf chasing fireflies under the moonlight. He sensed their urgency immediately and followed without question. Next, they located Thorn, the shy hedgehog, who had just finished settling into his new burrow with his family. Though hesitant, Thorn agreed to help, his trust in Baby giving him the courage to join.

With her team assembled, Baby led them back to the grove. Max sniffed the air, his golden eyes narrowing. "It smells...wrong here. Like the magic is fading."

"Can it do that?" Thorn asked, his small voice trembling.

"Magic isn't infinite," Pip explained, fluttering above the group. "It needs balance to thrive. If something's disrupting it, the whole forest could suffer."

Baby glanced at the ancient oak, determination shining in her eyes. "Then we need to find the source of the problem and fix it. Together."

The group began their search, fanning out across the grove to look for clues. Baby used her heightened senses to sniff for anything unusual, while Max's sharp vision scanned for disturbances. Pip flew above, watching for changes in the trees, and Thorn carefully inspected the ground, his small size allowing him to notice details the others might miss.

It was Thorn who discovered the first clue: a patch of ground near the oak tree where the soil was unnaturally dry and cracked, despite the recent rain. "Over here!" he squeaked, calling the others.

Baby padded over, her nose twitching as she sniffed the dry earth. "This doesn't belong here. The grove's magic keeps the soil rich and healthy."

Max scratched at the ground, uncovering a faint, dark residue that smelled faintly of metal. He growled. "Something's been here. Something that doesn't belong."

Pip landed beside the patch, his small nose wrinkling. "That's...not natural. It's like the magic's been drained."

Baby's collar pulsed faintly, its light reflecting off the residue. She took a deep breath, her mind racing. "Whatever caused this is still affecting the grove. We need to follow the trail."

The group followed the faint traces of residue through the forest, their journey leading them deeper into unfamiliar territory. The trees grew darker and more twisted, their branches forming claw-like shapes that cast eerie shadows. The air felt colder, and even Pip, usually full of snarky comments, was silent.

Finally, they came upon a clearing where the residue was strongest. At its center stood a strange, metallic object—a black, jagged shard that pulsed with an unnatural energy. The ground around it was barren, and the air hummed with a low, menacing vibration.

"What is that?" Thorn whispered, his spines bristling.

Max growled, his hackles rising. "Whatever it is, it's hurting the forest."

Baby stepped forward, her collar glowing brighter as she approached the shard. The closer she got, the more she felt its energy pulling at her, like a cold wind trying to snuff out a flame.

"We need to remove it," she said, her voice steady. "But it's too strong for one of us. We have to do this together."

The group quickly devised a plan. Pip would distract the shard's energy by flying in tight circles around it, his small, erratic movements drawing its focus. Thorn, with his tiny but strong claws, would dig around the shard to loosen it. Max, with his strength, would pull it free once it was dislodged. Baby would use her glowing collar to channel the grove's remaining magic, creating a barrier to protect her friends from the shard's harmful energy.

"Ready?" Baby asked, looking at each of them.

Pip saluted with a wing. "Let's do this."

Thorn nodded, his small body trembling but determined. Max let out a low growl, his golden eyes fierce. "We've got this."

The plan unfolded perfectly. Pip darted around the shard, his rapid movements causing its pulsing energy to waver. Thorn dug furiously, his tiny claws working faster than anyone expected. Max stepped in, gripping the shard with his powerful jaws and pulling with all his might.

Baby focused on her collar, its glow intensifying as she called upon the grove's magic. The light spread out in a shimmering wave, encircling her friends and shielding them from the shard's harmful energy. She could feel the strain, but she held steady, her determination unshakable.

With one final tug, Max yanked the shard free. A burst of dark energy shot out, but Baby's barrier held firm, dissipating the blast before it could reach them. The shard's pulsing light faded, and the forest seemed to let out a collective sigh of relief.

Carrying the shard, the group returned to the grove. The ancient oak tree seemed to sense their presence, its golden vines flickering with renewed hope. Baby placed the shard at the base of the tree, and together, they watched as the oak absorbed it, purifying its energy. The grove's light grew stronger, spreading out until the entire forest seemed to glow with life once more.

"You did it," Pip said, his voice full of awe. "We did it."

Thorn beamed, his spines relaxing. "The forest feels...happy again."

Max wagged his tail, his golden eyes shining. "That was amazing. We make a great team."

Baby looked at her friends, her heart swelling with pride. "We couldn't have done it without each other. The grove's magic is strong because it's about balance, just like us. When we work together, there's nothing we can't do."

As the first rays of dawn filtered through the trees, the group rested under the oak's glowing branches. The forest was safe, its magic restored, and Baby knew that their friendship was the greatest magic of all.

Chapter 12: Home Sweet Hollow

The morning after their daring rescue of the enchanted grove, the forest was alive with renewed energy. The leaves glistened with a golden dew, the trees swayed gently as if in gratitude, and the air buzzed with an invisible hum of magic restored. Baby stood at the edge of the grove, her glowing collar faintly pulsing in rhythm with the grove's light, a quiet smile on her face.

The adventure had been incredible, but Baby was ready to return to her cozy home with Lucy. She glanced at Pip, who perched on a nearby branch, and Max, who was chasing his tail in excitement over their victory. Thorn, the shy hedgehog, had already scampered back to his burrow, promising to visit soon.

"You're getting pretty good at this whole hero thing," Pip said, flapping down to land on Baby's head. "Not bad for a vampire pup."

Baby laughed, her tail wagging. "I couldn't have done it without you guys. We're a team."

Max bounded over, his golden eyes shining. "I still can't believe we saved the whole forest! The grove feels so much happier now."

"It's because we worked together," Baby said. "And because we believed in ourselves."

Max nodded solemnly, but Pip rolled his eyes. "Alright, enough of the sappy stuff. You've got a cozy bed and a doting human waiting for you. Let's head back to civilization before I get too used to this magical forest vibe."

As Baby made her way back to Moonlit Hollow, the familiar sights of her hometown filled her with warmth. The cobblestone streets sparkled in the sunlight, the cottages exuded their usual charm, and the townsfolk bustled about, preparing for the next community event. Though they had no idea of the adventures Baby had been on or the secrets she carried, their smiles and greetings made her feel truly at home.

When Baby trotted up to her front door, Lucy was already waiting, her face lighting up as she saw her beloved pup. "There you are! I was starting to worry."

Baby barked happily, running to Lucy and nuzzling her hand. Lucy knelt down to embrace her, burying her face in Baby's soft fur. "I don't know what you get up to out there, but you're always so full of life when you come home."

If only she knew, Baby thought with a chuckle. But Lucy's love and trust meant everything to her. She didn't need Lucy to know all her secrets to feel the warmth of their bond.

The day passed in a cozy haze of comfort. Lucy prepared Baby's favorite meal—a special dish of chicken and rice—while Baby lounged by the hearth, her tail thumping softly against the floor. Pip had returned to his favorite nook in the rafters, where he could keep an eye on everything while remaining out of sight. Max had wandered off to explore the forest, promising to visit the next time the moon was full.

As twilight fell and the first stars began to twinkle in the sky, Baby curled up on her blanket by the fireplace. Lucy sat nearby, reading a book, the soft glow of the lamp casting a golden light over the room. Everything felt peaceful, exactly as it should.

That night, Baby found herself reflecting on everything that had happened since she first discovered her vampire nature. From her playful escapades with Pip to their daring adventures in the forest, every moment had taught her something important. She had learned to embrace her differences, to use her powers responsibly, and to rely on her friends when the challenges grew too great to face alone.

But more than anything, she had learned that being different wasn't something to hide—it was something to celebrate. Her unique abilities had allowed her to help her friends, protect her home, and bring magic and joy to Moonlit Hollow. And while she might not always have the answers or know what lay ahead, she knew she was ready for whatever adventure came next.

As the moon rose high over Moonlit Hollow, Baby stepped outside onto the porch, her glowing collar softly lighting the steps. The town was quiet, the houses bathed in silver moonlight. She took a deep breath, the cool night air filling her lungs, and looked toward the forest. Somewhere out there, magic still lingered, and mysteries still waited to be uncovered.

Pip fluttered down from the porch railing, landing on Baby's back. "You thinking about another adventure already?"

Baby smiled, her tail wagging. "Not tonight. Tonight, I'm just enjoying being home."

Pip yawned, settling into the soft fur between her shoulders. "Good call. Even heroes need a break."

Baby chuckled, her gaze drifting to the stars. She thought about all the friends she had made—Max, Thorn, even the wise old owl Eldrin—and felt a surge of gratitude. They had shown her that no matter how different she might be, she was never alone.

As the clock struck midnight, Baby returned inside, her heart full and her spirit at peace. She curled up on her blanket by the fire, her collar glowing faintly in the darkness. Lucy leaned down to stroke her head, her voice soft and full of love.

"Goodnight, Baby. Sweet dreams."

And as Baby drifted off to sleep, she knew that her dreams would be filled with moonlit adventures, the laughter of friends, and the comforting knowledge that Moonlit Hollow would always be her home—a place where being different was her greatest strength and every night held the promise of something extraordinary.

Epilogue: A New Dawn Awaits

The soft crackle of the fireplace filled the cozy cottage as Moonlit Hollow drifted into slumber under the watchful glow of the full moon. Inside, Baby lay curled up on her favorite blanket near the hearth, her small chest rising and falling rhythmically as she relaxed after the day's excitement. Her sleek black-and-white fur shimmered faintly in the firelight, and her glowing collar pulsed gently, as if mirroring her dreams.

Lucy sat in the armchair nearby, her knitting needles clicking softly as she worked on a new scarf. Every now and then, she glanced at Baby with a warm smile, her heart full of affection for her extraordinary little companion. Though she couldn't explain it, Lucy always felt there was something magical about Baby—something beyond her intelligence and charm. But whatever it was, Lucy knew Baby was special, and that was enough.

Outside, the night was peaceful. The forest surrounding Moonlit Hollow stood tall and proud, its magic humming faintly, as if in gratitude for being restored. The town was quiet, its cobblestone streets bathed in silvery moonlight. Somewhere in the distance, the soft hoot of an owl and the rustle of leaves in the breeze hinted at the life that stirred after dark.

But inside the cottage, all was calm. The warmth of the fire, the gentle glow of Baby's collar, and the rhythmic clicking of Lucy's needles created a sense of serene contentment.

Baby shifted slightly, snuggling deeper into her blanket. Her dreams were vivid, a tapestry of the adventures she'd shared with her friends. She saw Pip flitting around the grove, his sarcastic wit bringing laughter to even the most tense moments. She saw Max bounding through the forest, his golden eyes shining with bravery and excitement. She saw Thorn, the shy hedgehog, standing tall despite his fears, proving that even the smallest among them could make a big difference.

But her dreams weren't just a reflection of the past—they hinted at what lay ahead. Baby could see the enchanted grove glowing brighter than ever, its golden vines stretching toward the sky as if inviting her back. She saw new paths winding through the forest, their secrets waiting to be uncovered. And beyond the forest, she glimpsed distant mountains and shimmering lakes, places she'd never explored but somehow knew were calling her.

In her dream, her collar glowed brighter, its crescent moon charm pulsing with energy. She felt a familiar hum of magic, but it was stronger now, more insistent. It was as if the collar itself was alive, whispering promises of new adventures, new challenges, and new friends to meet.

Lucy finished her knitting and set it aside, leaning down to stroke Baby's head. "Sweet dreams, Baby," she whispered, her voice soft and full of love. "Who knows what tomorrow will bring?"

Baby stirred slightly, letting out a contented sigh as her tail gave a small wag. Even in her sleep, she felt the warmth of Lucy's touch and the love that bound them together. It was this bond, Baby knew, that gave her the courage to embrace her differences and the strength to face whatever lay ahead.

As Lucy extinguished the fire and the cottage fell into darkness, Baby's collar flickered faintly, its glow casting a soft light across the room. The crescent moon charm shimmered for a brief moment, as if winking at the stars outside, before settling into a gentle pulse.

Somewhere in the distance, the first hints of dawn began to creep over the horizon, painting the sky in hues of deep indigo and soft gold. The forest stirred quietly, its magic humming in harmony with the awakening world. And as Baby lay curled up by the hearth, her dreams filled with moonlit adventures and the laughter of friends, the glowing collar around her neck seemed to whisper a quiet truth:

Her story was just beginning.

<u>Message from the Author:</u>

I hope you enjoyed this book, I love astrology and knew there was not a book such as this out on the shelf. I love metaphysical items as well. Please check out my other books:

-Life of Government Benefits

-My life of Hell

-My life with Hydrocephalus

-Red Sky

-World Domination:Woman's rule

-World Domination:Woman's Rule 2: The War

-Life and Banishment of Apophis: book 1

-The Kidney Friendly Diet

-The Ultimate Hemp Cookbook

-Creating a Dispensary(legally)

-Cleanliness throughout life: the importance of showering from childhood to adulthood.

-Strong Roots: The Risks of Overcoddling children

-Hemp Horoscopes: Cosmic Insights and Earthly Healing

- Celestial Hemp Navigating the Zodiac: Through the Green Cosmos

-Astrological Hemp: Aligning The Stars with Earth's Ancient Herb

-The Astrological Guide to Hemp: Stars, Signs, and Sacred Leaves

-Green Growth: Innovative Marketing Strategies for your Hemp Products and Dispensary

-Cosmic Cannabis

-Astrological Munchies

-Henry The Hemp

-Zodiacal Roots: The Astrological Soul Of Hemp

- **Green Constellations: Intersection of Hemp and Zodiac**

-Hemp in The Houses: An astrological Adventure Through The Cannabis Galaxy

-Galactic Ganja Guide

Heavenly Hemp

Zodiac Leaves

Doctor Who Astrology

Cannastrology

Stellar Satvias and Cosmic Indicas

Celestial Cannabis: A Zodiac Journey

AstroHerbology: The Sky and The Soil: Volume 1

AstroHerbology:Celestial Cannabis:Volume 2

Cosmic Cannabis Cultivation

The Starry Guide to Herbal Harmony: Volume 1

The Starry Guide to Herbal Harmony: Cannabis Universe: Volume 2

Yugioh Astrology: Astrological Guide to Deck, Duels and more

Nightmare Mansion: Echoes of The Abyss

Nightmare Mansion 2: Legacy of Shadows

Nightmare Mansion 3: Shadows of the Forgotten

Nightmare Mansion 4: Echoes of the Damned

The Life and Banishment of Apophis: Book 2

Nightmare Mansion: Halls of Despair

Healing with Herb: Cannabis and Hydrocephalus

Planetary Pot: Aligning with Astrological Herbs: Volume 1

Fast Track to Freedom: 30 Days to Financial Independence Using AI, Assets, and Agile Hustles

Cosmic Hemp Pathways

How to Become Financially Free in 30 Days: 10,000 Paths to Prosperity

Zodiacal Herbage: Astrological Insights: Volume 1

Nightmare Mansion: Whispers in the Walls

The Daleks Invade Atlantis

Henry the hemp and Hydrocephalus

10X The Kidney Friendly Diet

Cannabis Universe: Adult coloring book

Hemp Astrology: The Healing Power of the Stars

Zodiacal Herbage: Astrological Insights: Cannabis Universe: Volume 2

<u>Planetary Pot: Aligning with Astrological Herbs: Cannabis Universes: Volume 2</u>

Doctor Who Meets the Replicators and SG-1: The Ultimate Battle for Survival

Nightmare Mansion: Curse of the Blood Moon

<u>The Celestial Stoner: A Guide to the Zodiac</u>

Cosmic Pleasures: Sex Toy Astrology for Every Sign

Hydrocephalus Astrology: Navigating the Stars and Healing Waters

Lapis and the Mischievous Chocolate Bar

Celestial Positions: Sexual Astrology for Every Sign

Apophis's Shadow Work Journal: : A Journey of Self-Discovery and Healing

Kinky Cosmos: Sexual Kink Astrology for Every Sign

Digital Cosmos: The Astrological Digimon Compendium

Stellar Seeds: The Cosmic Guide to Growing with Astrology

Apophis's Daily Gratitude Journal

Cat Astrology: Feline Mysteries of the Cosmos

The Cosmic Kama Sutra: An Astrological Guide to Sexual Positions

Unleash Your Potential: A Guided Journal Powered by AI Insights

Whispers of the Enchanted Grove

Cosmic Pleasures: An Astrological Guide to Sexual Kinks

369, 12 Manifestation Journal

Whisper of the nocturne journal(blank journal for writing or drawing)

The Boogey Book

Locked In Reflection: A Chastity Journey Through Locktober

Generating Wealth Quickly:

How to Generate $100,000 in 24 Hours

Star Magic: Harness the Power of the Universe

The Flatulence Chronicles: A Fart Journal for Self-Discovery

The Doctor and The Death Moth

Seize the Day: A Personal Seizure Tracking Journal

The Ultimate Boogeyman Safari: A Journey into the Boogie World and Beyond

Whispers of Samhain: 1,000 Spells of Love, Luck, and Lunar Magic: Samhain Spell Book

Apophis's guides:

Witch's Spellbook Crafting Guide for Halloween

<u>Frost & Flame: The Enchanted Yule Grimoire of 1000 Winter Spells</u>

<u>The Ultimate Boogey Goo Guide & Spooky Activities for Halloween Fun</u>

Harmony of the Scales: A Libra's Spellcraft for Balance and Beauty

The Enchanted Advent: 36 Days of Christmas Wonders

Nightmare Mansion: The Labyrinth of Screams

Harvest of Enchantment: 1,000 Spells of Gratitude, Love, and Fortune for Thanksgiving

The Boogey Chronicles: A Journal of Nightly Encounters and Shadowy Secrets

The 12 Days of Financial Freedom: A Step-by-Step Christmas Countdown to Transform Your Finances

Sigil of the Eternal Spiral Blank Journal

A Christmas Feast: Timeless Recipes for Every Meal

Cosmic Sales: The Astrological Guide to Black Friday Shopping

Legends of the Corn Mother and Other Harvest Myths

Whispers of the Harvest: The Corn Mother's Journal

The Evergreen Spellbook

The Doctor Meets the Boogeyman

The White Witch of Rose Hall's SpellBook

The Gingerbread Golem's Shadow: A Study in Sweet Darkness

The Gingerbread Golem Codex: An Academic Exploration of Sweet Myths

The Gingerbread Golem Grimoire: Sweet Magicks and Spells for the Festive Witch

The Curse of the Gingerbread Golem

10-minute Christmas Crafts for kids

<u>Christmas Crisis Solutions: The Ultimate Last-Minute Survival Guide</u>

Gingerbread Golem Recipes: Holiday Treats with a Magical Twist

The Infinite Key: Unlocking Mystical Secrets of the Ages

Enchanted Yule: A Wiccan and Pagan Guide to a Magical and Memorable Season

Dinosaurs of Power: Unlocking Ancient Magick

Astro-Dinos: The Cosmic Guide to Prehistoric Wisdom

Gallifrey's Yule Logs: A Festive Doctor Who Cookbook

The Dino Grimoire: Secrets of Prehistoric Magick

The Gift They Never Knew They Needed

The Gingerbread Golem's Culinary Alchemy: Enchanting Recipes for a Sweetly Dark Feast

A Time Lord Christmas: Holiday Adventures with the Doctor

Krampusproofing Your Home: Defensive Strategies for Yule

Silent Frights: A Collection of Christmas Creepypastas to Chill Your Bones

Santa Raptor's Jolly Carnage: A Dino-Claus Christmas Tale

Prehistoric Palettes: A Dino Wicca Coloring Journey

The Christmas Wishkeeper Chronicles

The Starlight Sleigh: A Holiday Journey
Elf Secrets: The True Magic of the North Pole
Candy Cane Conjurations
Cooking with Kids: Recipes Under 20 Minutes
Doctor Who: The TARDIS Confiscation
The Anxiety First Aid Kit: Quick Tools to Calm Your Mind
Frosty Whispers: A Winter's Tale
The Infinite Key: Unlocking the Secrets to Prosperity, Resilience, and Purpose
The Grasping Void: Why You'll Regret This Purchase
Astrology for Busy Bees: Star Signs Simplified
The Instant Focus Formula: Cut Through the Noise
The Secret Language of Colors: Unlocking the Emotional Codes
Sacred Fossil Chronicles: Blank Journal
The Christmas Cottage Miracle
Feeding Frenzy: Graboid-Inspired Recipes
Manifest in Minutes: The Quick Law of Attraction Guide
The Symbiote Chronicles: Doctor Who's Venomous Journey
Think Tiny, Grow Big: The Minimalist Mindset
The Energy Key: Unlocking Limitless Motivation
New Year, New Magic: Manifesting Your Best Year Yet
Unstoppable You: Mastering Confidence in Minutes
Infinite Energy: The Secret to Never Feeling Drained
Lightning Focus: Mastering the Art of Productivity in a Distracted World
Saturnalia Manifestation Magick: A Guide to Unlocking Abundance During the Solstice
Graboids and Garland: The Ultimate Tremors-Themed Christmas Guide
12 Nights of Holiday Magic
The Power of Pause: 60-Second Mindfulness Practices
The Quick Reset: How to Reclaim Your Life After Burnout
The Shadow Eater: A Tale of Despair and Survival

The Micro-Mastery Method: Transform Your Skills in Just Minutes a Day

Reclaiming Time: How to Live More by Doing Less

Chronovore: The Eternal Nexus

The Mind Reset: Unlocking Your Inner Peace in a Chaotic World

Confidence Code: Building Unshakable Self-Belief

If you want solar for your home go here: https://www.harborsolar.live/apophisenterprises/

Get Some Tarot cards: https://www.makeplayingcards.com/sell/apophis-occult-shop

Get some shirts: https://www.bonfire.com/store/apophis-shirt-emporium/

<u>**Instagrams:**</u>
@apophis_enterprises,
@apophisbookemporium,
@apophisscardshop
Twitter: @apophisenterpr1
 Tiktok:@apophisenterprise
Youtube: @sg1fan23477, @FiresideRetreatKingdom
Hive: @sg1fan23477
CheeLee: @SG1fan23477

Podcast: Apophis Chat Zone: https://open.spotify.com/show/5zXbrCLEV2xzCp8ybrfHsk?si=fb4d4fdbdce44dec

Newsletter: https://apophiss-newsletter-27c897.beehiiv.com/

If you want to support me or see posts of other projects that I have come over to: **buymeacoffee.com/mpetchinskg**

I post there daily several times a day

Get your Dinowicca or Christmas themed digital products, especially Santa Raptor songs and other musics. Here: **https://sg1fan23477.gumroad.com**

Apophis Yuletide Digital has not only digital Christmas items, but it will have all things with Dinowicca as well as other Digital products.